Sedina ♡

Here are some other Redfeather Books you will enjoy

* *Alvin's Famous No-Horse*
by William Harry Harding

* *The Class with the Summer Birthdays*
by Dian Curtis Regan

* *The Curse of the Trouble Dolls*
by Dian Curtis Regan

Lavender
by Karen Hesse

T. WHITE

Sable
by Karen Hesse

* *Snakes Are Nothing to Sneeze At*
by Gabrielle Charbonnet

T. ANDERSON

* *Stargone John*
by Ellen Kindt McKenzie

Tutu Much Ballet
by Gabrielle Charbonnet

* *Twin Surprises*
by Susan Beth Pfeffer

* *Twin Troubles*
by Susan Beth Pfeffer

* *Available in paperback*

Dian Curtis Regan

THE PEPPERMINT RACE

illustrated by Anna Dewdney

A REDFEATHER BOOK

Henry Holt and Company · *New York*

To all the kids who ring my doorbell,
knowing I will buy whatever
kind of candy they are selling

—D. C. R.

To Berol, who draws with Mommy

—A. D.

Henry Holt and Company, Inc.
Publishers since 1866
115 West 18th Street
New York, New York 10011
Henry Holt is a registered trademark of Henry Holt and Company, Inc.
Text copyright ©1994 by Dian Curtis Regan
Illustrations copyright © 1994 by Anna Dewdney. All rights reserved.
Published in Canada by Fitzhenry & Whiteside Ltd.,
195 Allstate Parkway, Markham, Ontario L3R 4T8.
Library of Congress Cataloging-in-Publication Data
Regan, Dian Curtis. The peppermint race / Dian Curtis Regan;
illustrated by Anna Dewdney. p.   cm.—(A Redfeather book)
Summary: Tony hopes to win the first pick of prizes in his school's fund-raiser,
but he discovers that selling candy is not as easy as he had thought,
especially when another fourth grader also wants to win.
[1. Contests—Fiction. 2. Schools—Fiction.] I. Dewdney, Anna, ill. II. Title. III. Series:
Redfeather books. PZ7.R25854Pe   1994   [Fic]—dc20   94-6833
ISBN 0-8050-2753-X (hardcover)
1   3   5   7   9   10   8   6   4   2
ISBN 0-8050-4675-5 (paperback)
1   3   5   7   9   10   8   6   4   2
First published in hardcover in 1994 by Henry Holt and Company, Inc.
First Redfeather paperback edition, 1996
Printed in the United States of America on acid-free paper. ∞

Contents

THE PEPPERMINT RACE

1

The Almost Empty Library

"They're here! They're here!"

Tony Adler jumped as Veronica Tangle's screechy voice broke the "Quiet!" rule in the school's new library.

Mr. Peek's head appeared between the floppy ears of a stuffed rabbit who wore reading glasses and held a copy of *Peter Rabbit* in its paws.

"*What's* here?" he rasped in the loud whisper only librarians use. His tiny reading glasses matched the rabbit's.

"The peppermints came, and—"

"Shhh!" Glaring at Veronica, Mr. Peek stepped around the rabbit, shuffling a stack of books in his hands. "This is a library, Miss Tangle. We do not yell in a library."

Tony snickered as quietly as he could. Mr. Peek loved

to say "This is a library." He must think fourth graders needed to be reminded every Monday and Thursday what this room for books was called.

Veronica gave a loud sigh, as if it was impossible to announce the arrival of the peppermints in any voice lower than a shout. "Miss Kimball needs two more helpers to carry boxes." She shoved up owl-eye glasses, which made her ears stick out through her pixie haircut.

Twenty-five hands shot up.

Veronica fixed a fist on each hip the way Miss Kimball did when she chose helpers. "Umm," she ummed.

"Well, *choose*," urged Mr. Peek, polishing the check-out counter with the sleeve of his fuzzy sweater. He acted proud of his new library, which had been built onto the school during summer vacation.

The *problem* with the library was that most of the shelves were empty—even now in December, after each grade had donated books from class libraries and brought used ones from home.

"I chooooose . . ." Veronica began.

Tony raised to his toes, making his arm tower above the others.

Beside him his friend Jeremy Nix did the same. "Uh, uh," he grunted.

Jeremy pretended to be in great pain whenever he wanted to get chosen for something, as if the chooser might feel sorry for him.

"Erica and Ann," Veronica finished.

"Ewww," Jeremy groaned.

Tony agreed with Jeremy. Yet he'd known all along that Veronica would choose her own friends. He shouldn't have bothered to raise his hand.

The clicking of Miss Kimball's heels echoed in the hallway. Stepping into the library, she paused, giving her blond hair a shake as she beamed at Mr. Peek.

The librarian yanked off his glasses, smoothed his sweater, and returned her beam.

The girls tittered and elbowed each other. They liked to whisper about the teacher and the librarian being *in love*.

Tony thought it was stupid. Why did two grown-ups smiling at each other mean they were *in love*?

"Oh, Mr. Peek," the teacher gushed, placing a timid hand against one cheek. "Thank you for helping my kids choose books."

"Any time," he answered in his whisper-voice. "*Any* time."

They kept gazing at each other, like they were acting out a love scene in a mushy movie.

Tony glanced away, embarrassed for them. Didn't they notice everyone staring?

"Line up," Miss Kimball finally said. "I need a leader to take the class back. My helpers"—she nodded at Veronica and her friends—"will be there in a minute with a *big* surprise."

"We already know," Jeremy blurted. "Veronica told us."

Miss Kimball's beam faded. "I *told* you it was a secret."

Veronica dipped her head and balanced on one leg, as if that might distract the teacher long enough to forgive and forget.

Meanwhile, twenty-three hands waved wildly.

"Uh, uh," grunted Jeremy.

"Okay, Jeremy," Miss Kimball said. "You're in charge."

Tony laughed as his friend made a goofy face. The agony act had worked this time.

As Jeremy rounded up the class, Tony hurried to check out a book. Even though the library's selection was dismal, he'd requested mysteries by his favorite author, Zelda Mask.

Mr. Peek had gotten them. Just for Tony.

The librarian stamped Tony's book, *Mystery of the Dragon King*, and slipped a card into the pocket. "Thanks to the peppermints," Mr. Peek whispered, "we'll soon have a whole shelf of Zelda Mask mysteries."

"Really?" Tony had already read seven of them. Yesterday Mr. Peek showed him how to scan titles on the computer screen. Thirty-three. Tony wanted to read every one.

"We'll have the books, that is—" Mr. Peek paused to wave at Jeremy, dismissing the class. "If you sell lots and *lots* of peppermints before Christmas."

"I will," Tony promised.

He glanced at the library's display case. A sign read: THE FOURTH GRADE PEPPERMINT RACE. Glistening under a spotlight were prizes for those who sold the most candy: a skateboard, computer games, puzzles, cassette tapes, Rollerblades, and other prizes, including the one Tony wanted most of all.

He focused on it. A candy-apple-red guitar. The

spotlight reflected off it so brightly, he could see his own face when he got close.

The guitar was electric, and came with a tiny Pignose amp. A decal next to the tuning pegs read: STAR-CATCHER.

Tony couldn't play very well, but he was learning. His uncle had been teaching him chords and simple songs.

Uncle John played in a band called the Burnt Spyders. His black guitar was dented, scratched, and scuffed, like an old pair of Sunday dress-up shoes.

The guitar once belonged to a famous musician. And even though Tony thought it was ugly, Uncle John could make it sound brand-new when his fingers danced upon the strings, making them whine and sing.

Tony wanted to make the strings sing too. But he wanted to learn on a shiny new guitar that he won for selling the most peppermints.

"Come on!" Jeremy snapped his fingers three times in Tony's face. "And stop gaping at the skateboard. It's mine."

Tony peeled his attention away from the prize case and hustled to catch up with his friend. "I already have a skateboard."

"Well, I don't."

Jeremy was a terrific skateboarder, but his had been stolen. He couldn't get another one until he earned the money to pay for it, according to his parents.

He nudged Tony out the door. "Get going. The line's already gone."

"So who made *you* teacher?"

"Miss Kimball." Jeremy fluttered his eyelashes, and placed a timid hand on one cheek. "Oh, Mr. Peek, thank you for helping my kids choose books," he singsonged.

"Stop it." Tony jabbed him with the library book, then trotted back to class. He wanted to get there in time to grab as many boxes of peppermints as he could carry.

He, Anthony Adler, vowed to sell more peppermints than anyone else in the fourth grade.

For Zelda Mask mysteries for the new library.

And for his candy-apple-red guitar.

2

The Dragon King

Tony read *Mystery of the Dragon King* while waiting for the peppermints to arrive. His eyes raced over the words, trying to spot as many clues as he could before Miss Kimball interrupted.

How had a dragon become king of Cromwell Castle? The peasants feared its fire-licking roar and its massive strength. Worst of all, the dragon was holding their beloved princess captive.

"Books closed," came Miss Kimball's voice as she stepped into the room.

Tony was concentrating so hard on the story, he hadn't heard the clicking of the teacher's heels. Behind her, Erica, Ann, and Veronica paraded through the door, then piled boxes of peppermints on a long table in the back.

"We'll start by assigning five boxes to everyone," Miss Kimball began, tearing one open. The tangy smell of peppermint drifted across the room.

"Each box holds twenty bags of candy. And look." She held one up. "They're decorated with four holiday designs. Who could resist buying these to help our library?"

"How much money will we make?" Jeremy asked.

Veronica gave a loud *tsk-sigh*, as though she thought it was a stupid question. "It depends on how many bags you sell."

"He *meant* how much do we charge." Tony wrinkled his lip at her, defending his friend.

"Yeah." Jeremy *tsk-sigh*ed like Veronica was the stupid one.

"Each bag is a dollar," Miss Kimball answered. "So you'll collect twenty dollars for every box you sell."

She hurried to the front of the room, taking tiny steps. Tony wondered how she could walk in such silly shoes. "Thanks to Erica and Ann," the teacher said, "we can chart everyone's progress on our candy graph."

Sliding a pink poster from behind a cabinet, Miss Kimball balanced it on the chalk tray. The outline of a giant peppermint piece surrounded their names. The

letters were colored in red-and-white stripes like candy canes.

"When you sell a whole box," the teacher said, "a real peppermint piece will be taped next to your name."

Cool, Tony thought, joining in as a few kids clapped. Erica and Ann looked pleased. They both sported a bump in one cheek. Had they gotten into the candy already?

Squinting at the graph, Tony pictured five peppermint pieces after his name—one for each box. Then he pictured himself playing the red guitar. Maybe he'd even start his own band: Tony and the Peppermints—ha!

Setting aside his book, he grabbed a pencil and scribbled numbers on the palm of his hand. How much money would he make for the library by selling all five boxes?

$$
\begin{array}{r}
20 \text{ bags} \\
\times\ 5 \text{ boxes} \\
\hline
100 \text{ dollars}
\end{array}
$$

A hundred dollars! That would buy a lot of Zelda Mask books. And it would surely win him the guitar.

"Remember," Miss Kimball said. "The easiest sales will be to relatives and neighbors who know you."

"My grandmother said she'd buy four bags!" cried Veronica.

"Wow," came a few scattered voices.

"Who can remember our three rules?" Miss Kimball asked. "Tony?"

"Ummm." Tony had been sneaking peeks at his *Dragon King* book, so he had to stop and think. "Tell customers how the money will be spent."

"Right," Miss Kimball said. "And rule number two?"

"Uh, uh."

"Jeremy?"

"Make sure your parents know where you are."

"Good. Rule three?"

"Be polite," Veronica finished without waiting to be called on.

Tony thought Veronica could use a lesson in politeness, the way she gave answers and opinions without raising her hand.

"Any questions?"

"When will we get the prizes?" Erica asked, cupping one palm over her cheek so the teacher wouldn't notice she was eating candy.

"On Friday, before we break for the holidays."

Whispers exploded around the room:

"I want the space game."

"I'm getting the Rollerblades."

"No, *I'm* getting the Rollerblades."

"Well, I want the jet car set."

"The skateboard's mine." That was Jeremy.

Someone claimed the guitar.

In the jumble of whispers bumping and sliding into each other, Tony wasn't sure who said it. But it made him more determined than ever to win.

The bell rang.

"Take your boxes as you leave," Miss Kimball called. "And good luck. Here's to *lots* of new books for Philip— uh, I mean for Mr. Peek—uh, I mean for the *library*."

Ducking her head, she *click-click*ed to her desk.

The class dashed to grab boxes and coats, spilling hats and gloves across the floor.

"I get Astor Street!" someone shouted, racing out the door.

"Waverly Place is mine."

"Stay away from Eighteenth."

"You can't have the whole street."

"I can too. I live on it."

"So? I'll beat you there."

Tony shoved five boxes into his book bag along with *Dragon King*. He'd better take the shortcut home to save time. No one was going to ace *him* out of his own neighborhood before he got there.

As he dashed across the playground, his shoes pounded against the frozen dirt in rhythm:

The pep-per-mint race has be-gun.
The pep-per-mint race has be-gun.

3

First Sale

Tony missed walking home from school with Jeremy. The Nix family had moved to a new house so far away, Jeremy now had to ride the bus.

The only time Tony saw his friend was at school, which meant walking home was usually boring. Today, however, was *not* boring. Tony was glad to be alone, so he could hurry.

Running down an alley behind the playground, Tony cut across a grassy hill that sloped to the front drive of the Eldercare Center. He caught sight of Mr. Ramirez, bushy silver hair bright in the cold afternoon sun. The man circled the hill on the paved pathway every day—rain, snow, or sunshine.

Usually Tony stopped to talk. Mr. Ramirez had lots of opinions on "what schools should be teaching you kids," but today Tony was in a rush to get home and start looking for customers.

Customers.

Tony put on the brakes. Why couldn't Mr. Ramirez be his first customer?

"Hey!" he called, waving.

The old man stopped and shaded his eyes. "Anthony Adler!" he hollered back. "Come tell me about your day."

Tony jogged across the grass to the pathway, feeling excited. He hoped he remembered everything he was supposed to say. Dumping his book bag on the path, he unzipped it and yanked out a box of candy.

"What've you got there?" Mr. Ramirez tilted his head to look through his bifocals. The wind caught his scarf, unwinding it from his shoulders.

"Christmas candy," Tony said, reaching to catch the scarf. "My class is selling peppermints to buy books for our new library."

"Candy for books, huh?" Mr. Ramirez pulled off a glove and unbuttoned his coat, digging into a pocket. "Well, that sounds like a good cause. Give me one." He handed Tony a quarter.

"Um." Tony didn't know what to say. Maybe he

should show Mr. Ramirez how big the bag was, so he'd know it cost more than a quarter.

Tony tore open the box and pulled out a bag. It was decorated with reindeer sporting red bows and sleigh bells on their harnesses.

The bag was not very big. Actually, it was quite small.

"Here's your candy, sir, but it costs, um, a dollar."

"A *dollar?*" The man's bushy eyebrows shot above his glasses. "This little thing costs a dollar?"

Tony nodded. "It's for books, sir, for our library," he added, reminding Mr. Ramirez that he'd said it was a good cause.

Tony had planned to tell him about the guitar, too, but maybe he shouldn't mention it. What if only *half* the money went to the library, and the other half paid for the prizes? Mr. Ramirez might not think prizes were a good cause.

The man dug into his pocket again, then clinked another quarter and a fifty-cent piece into Tony's hand.

Tony slipped the money into a special envelope Miss Kimball had given him. He'd have to remember to put an X on it when he got home, because he didn't have a pencil right now.

He handed the bag to Mr. Ramirez. "The peppermints are really delicious," he said. "You'll love them." The minute the words fell out of his mouth, he wondered why he said them. He'd never *tasted* the peppermints.

Mr. Ramirez buttoned his coat, shoved the bag into a pocket, and continued on his way. Tony could hear him mumbling "A dollar a bag" as he walked.

Gathering his things, Tony dashed home. He felt guilty taking Mr. Ramirez's money. But if Miss Kimball said the candy cost a dollar, then that's what he had to charge. Was it his fault the bags were so tiny?

He bounded up the steps to apartment D 205. Inside, he dialed his mom's work number—their daily ritual. She wasn't at her desk, so Tony left a message saying he'd be selling peppermints until dinnertime.

Maybe he should start inside his apartment building. That way he could keep warm while he went door to door. He hoped he didn't run into Veronica Tangle, because she lived in the D building too.

Tony wiggled out of his jacket, pulled a box and the special envelope from his book bag, then opened the door. Wait a minute. Shouldn't he *taste* the candy before telling customers it was delicious?

What if it wasn't? What if the candy maker had used salt instead of sugar, like his mom did one time when she made fudge?

What if the peppermints tasted awful?

Closing the door, he helped himself to a bag. This one was decorated with spiky green holly and mistletoe with white berries. Tony hesitated. He couldn't rip it open, eat one peppermint, then tape the bag shut and sell it.

He'd have to buy the whole bag. So what? It was a sale, wasn't it? Whether he or somebody else bought it? A dollar's a dollar.

He hurried into his bedroom, opening the blinds to let in daylight. He kept the blinds shut so his pet gerbil, Toxic, could nap in the afternoon.

Toxic was named after Tony's favorite band. A poster of the group decorated the back of his door. The four guys leaned against a brick wall next to their guitars. They posed unsmiling, with arms crossed. That's how

Tony posed for pictures now too, and it drove his mother crazy.

He checked on his gerbil. The furry ball was asleep under a lettuce leaf, so Tony didn't bother him.

Kneeling on the bed, he lifted his football bank off the shelf above the headboard. He'd been saving his allowance for Christmas presents, but it wouldn't hurt to borrow one dollar.

Besides, he'd already bought a couple of gifts. For his mom, he'd bought Dentelle Noire perfume. The bottle was wrapped in black lace, which is what the words meant in French, according to the label.

And for Uncle John, Tony had bought a box of multicolored guitar picks because his uncle was always losing them.

Tony had one more gift to save for—Jeremy's. He couldn't think of anything good to get his friend. But there was still time.

Pulling the cork from the bottom of the bank, Tony shook out coins until they totaled a dollar. Then he slipped the money into the special envelope. Finding a pencil, he marked two Xs—one for his bag and one for Mr. Ramirez's.

Lying on his bed, Tony ate one peppermint after another. They weren't awful at all. They were scrumptious. Sweet and minty.

Good. Now he could recommend the candy to his customers and mean it.

Tony reached for another piece. He twisted the wrapper off and popped it into his mouth. The cool peppermint flavor tickled his throat. He sucked on it for a minute, then crunched and swallowed.

He took another piece to study. It looked like a mini candy cane, only fatter. He popped it into his mouth and reached for one more.

The bag was empty. Tony jumped off the bed. Had he eaten a whole bag in three minutes? That *wasn't* much candy for one dollar. Mr. Ramirez was right to complain.

He shook more coins out of his bank, popped the cork in, and returned the bank to its shelf. Then he helped himself to a second bag and put another X on the envelope.

While he snacked, Tony sprinkled sunflower seeds into Toxic's dish. Lifting the lettuce leaf, he petted the charcoal-and-white dappled head with one finger.

When the second bag was empty, he gathered his

things together and hurried from the apartment, ready to get down to business.

Tasting the candy put Tony into a good mood. He'd already sold three bags, and school hadn't even been out one hour!

"Not bad," he mumbled as he hurried down the hall. "Not bad at all."

He tried to ignore the fact that two of the sales had been to himself.

4

Business Booms—Sort of

Tony stared at the door of apartment 206.

Do it, he told himself. *Knock.*

He knocked.

The door opened. Mrs. Trevino smiled at him. She was a model. Tony thought she was pretty, with her perfect white smile and smooth dark skin.

"Tony!" she exclaimed. "What do you need today?"

The only time he knocked on her door was when his mom needed to borrow something.

"Nothing," he stammered. "I mean . . ." *Stop stammering*, he told himself. "I'm selling peppermints so my school can buy books for our new library."

"How much?"

Tony cocked his head. "A dollar?" He watched her face, but she didn't frown like Mr. Ramirez. "The packages are tiny, though," he added, kicking at the door frame, "so if you—"

"Don't move." In a few seconds she was back with her purse. "One dollar." She handed it over with a camera-pleasing smile.

"Thank you!" Tony slipped the money into the envelope and marked another X in the neat row he'd started. She didn't mind paying a dollar at all. "Thank you very, very much," he said, rushing toward the next apartment.

"Tony?" Mrs. Trevino called.

He stopped. Did she want to buy another bag? So soon?

"Where are my peppermints?"

"Whoops!" Tony felt his face flush. Rushing back, he gave her a bag decorated with lacy snowflakes and dripping icicles. "I'm sorry," he said, feeling dumb.

"It's okay." She wiggled the bag, making it crinkle. "Good luck with your project."

"Thanks."

This is easy, Tony sang to himself. Stopping at the next door, he gave it a bold knock.

"Who's there?" came a grumbly voice.

Tony cleared his throat. "Tony Adler from 205," he called.

The door opened a crack. Mr. and Mrs. Webb peeked out. Her head appeared above his, since she towered over him.

The Webbs didn't have children. From the way they were glowering at Tony, he wondered if they *liked* children.

"What do you want?" demanded Mrs. Webb.

"Well," Tony began, hearing his voice quiver. "My school is sell—"

"Speak up, young man," snapped Mr. Webb.

"Yes, sir." Tony began again, a bit louder: "My school is selling peppermints for—"

"It's another one," Mrs. Webb interrupted, stepping out of sight behind the door. "Call the super and tell him we've got another door-to-door salesman."

"Martha, he's just a kid."

"I don't care. It's a rule. No solicitors. That's one of the reasons we moved here."

"It's for books, ma'am."

"What?" The door opened wider. Mrs. Webb peered at him.

"The money is for books for our new library."

"I don't care, young man. If I say yes to you, why,

tomorrow I'll have ten more people knocking on my door, asking for money."

"Sorry to bother you." Tony clutched the box to his chest and backed away.

"Martha, it's for *books*," Mr. Webb was saying as the door slammed.

Tony ran down a flight of stairs and faced apartment 107. His heart pounded. *Win a few, lose a few.* That's what Uncle John said when the Burnt Spyders lost an audition.

Tony didn't know who lived in 107. He knocked anyway.

A lady holding a baby on one hip opened the door. A toddler peeked between her legs. From another room came the sound of a third child, crying.

"Yes?" She seemed as grumpy as Mrs. Webb as she tried to finger-comb her messed-up hair.

"My school is selling peppermints—"

"Candy!" the toddler shrieked, grabbing boldly for the bag Tony held.

The lady wasn't too pleased about Tony letting her son see the bag. "How much?"

"Only a dollar," Tony said with enthusiasm, as if it was a bargain.

"Can you come in a minute?" she asked, pulling the toddler inside.

Tony stepped in and shut the door.

"Do you live in the apartments?"

"Yes, upstairs in 205." Tony set the box of candy on a sofa and got out his envelope. "I'm Tony Adler."

"Nice to meet you." She sat the baby on a yellow blanket crumpled in a heap on the floor, then straightened her clothes. "I'm Sara Glenn. This is Peter, baby Christopher, and the one you can hear but not see is Rosie."

"Hi," Tony said to the kids.

Mrs. Glenn took the bag. It was decorated with snow-covered pines and twinkly white stars. She carried it into the kitchen and set it on top of the refrigerator in spite of the fact that Peter was screaming, "Mine, mine, mine!"

"Later," she told him. "After dinner."

Peter burst into tears and scampered away.

"Will you keep an eye on the baby for a second while I find a dollar?"

"Sure," Tony said.

Mrs. Glenn disappeared down the hallway. The baby squealed and started after her.

"Hey, Christopher." Tony dropped to his knees beside the blanket. He stretched out the corners and smoothed it flat. "Look." He shook a walrus rattle while the baby watched, chewing one fist.

Mrs. Glenn returned and gave him a dollar.

"Thank you." Tony put the money away and marked the envelope. Heading for the door, he grabbed the box from the sofa. An unwrapped peppermint lay on the cushion. Another was on the floor.

Tony twirled, searching for Peter. He crouched in the kitchen. Wet peppermint pieces stuck to both hands. Candy smeared his chin.

"Peter!" cried Mrs. Glenn. "Oh, Tony, I'm sorry."

"It's okay." He sighed. What else could he say?

"That was my last dollar. Can you come back tomorrow? I'll pay for the other bag then."

"Sure." Tony tried to feel pleased about selling two bags. But he didn't. Not when Mrs. Glenn felt obligated to buy the second one.

He said good-bye, ignoring Peter's sticky wave as he left.

Tony's stomach told him it was time to go home for dinner. He didn't want to be late, or his mom might not let him sell candy tomorrow.

He ran up the steps to his apartment. Inside, Mom was setting the table for dinner, still dressed in her red suit, minus the heels and earrings.

"Hi, honey," she said. "Have any luck selling candy?" She folded a napkin beside each plate.

"Sort of."

"Let me hear your sales pitch."

"Good evening, ma'am," Tony said in his brightest voice. "Dinner smells wonderful, and you look very pretty."

She laughed. "Flattery will not raise your allowance." Pouring a glass of milk, she set it by his plate. "Tell me what you *really* say."

Tony showed her a bag. "I say, my school is selling peppermints to buy books for our new library. Would you like some?"

"Yes."

"You would?"

His mom pulled some dollars from the wooden cat canister where she stored her grocery money. "Two, please."

"Wow." Tony fetched her a second bag. "You're the easiest customer I've had all day."

That is, he added to himself, *next to me.*

5

The Candy Graph Doesn't Lie

Tony could hardly get to sleep.

After dinner, Grandmother Adler called. Tony sold her four bags of peppermints over the phone. *Four!* The same number Veronica sold *her* grandmother.

Then Tony called Uncle John. He bought *two* bags. Tony told him about the candy-apple-red guitar, and how he planned to win it.

Uncle John promised to teach him the A minor and G7 chords so he could play "Jolly Old Saint Nicholas." He already knew the other chords in the song.

No wonder Tony was still awake at midnight. He'd counted dollars and Xs on the envelope over and over to make sure they came out right.

Fourteen Xs. Thirteen dollars—thanks to Mrs. Glenn.

In the morning, Tony ran all the way to school. He

couldn't wait to find out if he'd sold more candy than anyone else.

Miss Kimball was at her desk tallying Xs and dollars while Ann and Erica taped peppermints onto the candy graph—and sneaked pieces for themselves when the teacher wasn't looking.

Tony searched for his name on the graph as he carried his envelope to the teacher's desk. He explained the missing dollar, then hovered over her shoulder, scanning the NUMBER OF BAGS SOLD column.

Numbers jumped off the page and socked him in the eyeball.

Numbers like nineteen. Twenty-eight. Forty-one.

Forty-one? Who'd sold *that* many the first day?

"Sit down," Miss Kimball told him before he could see the name.

As he sat, he remembered the number needed to get a candy piece. Twenty bags. A whole box. He hadn't earned even *one* piece.

Tony waited until Ann and Erica finished taping. The person who'd sold forty-one bags and earned two candy pieces was Veronica Tangle. He should have guessed.

At least he wasn't the only one who hadn't made it onto the candy graph. Jeremy had sold only ten bags.

With five brothers and sisters, he had a lot of customers under his own roof—but not many neighbors. Not in his new neighborhood.

Mr. Peek tapped on the door, squinting at Miss Kimball because he didn't have his glasses on. "How'd we do the first day?"

She brightened at the sight of the librarian, motioning him to her desk. As they bent over the figures, sounds of giggling skittered across the room, along with a few groans.

Tony ignored the whisperings, using the opportunity to return to his *Dragon King* book:

Sir Perry saw it again. A beautiful face. A sad face. Gazing from the turret of Cromwell Castle into the darkness where he hid.

It had to be the princess. The princess the Dragon King captured fifteen years ago, on the day she was born. Sir Perry was a lad then, but he clearly remembered the day it happened.

Well, he would fight the Dragon King. With sword and skill, learned from his apprenticeship with Master Trivian. He would free the captured princess. The sad beautiful princess. Then his kingdom would no longer live in fear.

"Anthony Adler," Miss Kimball said, calling roll.

Mr. Peek was walking backward to the door, as if he couldn't bear to tear his eyes off Miss Kimball until he absolutely had to.

"Here," Tony answered, reluctantly closing the mystery book. He was eager to get to the good part. The part where Sir Perry ambushed the Dragon King. He hoped the battle was long and bloody.

But Zelda Mask was spending an awful lot of time on this captured-princess thing. Tony didn't like it. His favorite author was turning mushy on him. And—between Mr. Peek and Miss Kimball—he'd had enough mush to last him till Christmas.

At lunch Tony and Jeremy started to sit at their usual table. But Erica and Ann were there, borrowing apples off everyone's tray. They twisted the stems, chanting names of boys with each twist to see whose name broke the stem. It predicted who they would marry—or so they said.

The boys groaned, and chose another table. Unfortunately, Veronica was there.

"I sold more peppermints than anyone," she bragged, "in our class and in the other fourth grade."

"So?" Tony said. "It's only the first day. Your customers probably knew you, but now you have to sell to complete strangers. It's not easy." Tony thought of the Webbs and how they'd slammed the door in his face.

"You're just jealous," Veronica said, spearing a green bean with her fork. "You'll see. I'm going to win. Then I get to choose the prize I want."

"Which one will you pick?" asked Jeremy, even though Tony jabbed him to keep quiet. He didn't care which prize Veronica chose, as long as it wasn't—

"The red guitar," she answered with a flippy smirk.

6

Candy Boy

Tony could barely wait for the dismissal bell. His mind was already out the door, dashing across the playground, tearing past the Eldercare Center, racing home to sell peppermints.

How could Veronica possibly want the red guitar? *His* guitar. There were lots of other nifty prizes. Why did *that* have to be the one she chose? And how could she have sold forty-one bags of peppermints the first day?

The final bell rang.

Tony was off, following the path he'd run inside his mind.

Flying down the slope by the Eldercare Center, he waved at Mr. Ramirez. No time today to stop and chat.

Wait. Tony slowed to a jog. The Eldercare Center

was full of people, wasn't it? Customers. Had anyone else in the fourth grade thought of it?

He walked up the front drive to the entryway, catching his breath while smoothing his hair. Why not try?

Inside, about twenty senior citizens filled a cozy reception area, reading, watching TV, napping, or visiting. The room smelled of furniture polish and potpourri, and looked like somebody's living room, with lots of chairs, couches, tables, and pictures of flowers on the walls.

A nurse in a plaid uniform sat in a cubicle next to the door. Tony thought it best to ask permission before selling the candy, so he explained his visit to her.

She shoved a pencil behind one ear. "Try, if you'd like," she told him.

Tony cleared his throat. "What about you, ma'am?"

She peered at him.

"Would you like to buy some peppermints?"

"Ha," she answered. "And blow my diet? No, thank you." The nurse moved to answer a phone, so Tony stepped into the reception area.

He repeated his speech over and over to each group. For some, he almost had to shout it until they heard.

After his eighteenth try, he'd sold only three bags.

Everyone *oh*ed and *ah*ed over the brightly decorated candy, acting as if they truly wanted a bag. But no one seemed to have any money.

Tony felt bad. His great idea was *not* working.

As he was leaving, he noticed a decorative holiday bowl sitting empty on a coffee table. Tony stopped to pour a bag of peppermints into the dish. They barely covered the bottom.

He ripped open another bag and dumped the candy into the bowl. It still looked like a puny amount. Tony sighed, adding a third bag.

Three more dollars from his football bank. Selling peppermints was beginning to cost him a lot of money.

At home, after calling his mom's office, he visited the rest of the apartments in his building. At every door he gave his speech, adding little extras like: "They make great stocking stuffers!" or "Kids love them!"

But every almost-customer told him that someone had been there before him, selling peppermints.

Someone like Veronica Tangle.

If only he hadn't stopped at the Eldercare Center, he would have beat Veronica home, made more sales—and been three dollars richer.

Tony stopped at Mrs. Glenn's door and knocked. He could hear at least two of her kids crying.

Peter opened the door. "Candy boy!" he cried when he saw Tony.

Ha, Tony laughed to himself. *Candy boy. That's me.*

The door opened wider. Mrs. Glenn did *not* seem to be in a very good mood. "How many of you kids are going to knock on my door selling candy?"

Uh, oh. Veronica strikes again. "Um, I came to collect the dollar you owe me," Tony said. "You told me to come back today, remember?"

"So I did." Mrs. Glenn unwound Peter from her leg. "Well, I gave your dollar to a girl with real short hair and big round glasses. She said she knew you, and promised to give you the dollar tomorrow."

"Oh." Tony wished Veronica had minded her own business.

The door closed. He went back to his apartment to get a jacket and gloves. It was time to try the rest of the neighborhood.

An hour later he'd made only five sales. Five. In a whole hour.

Someone had beat him to almost every house. Tony hoped it was other kids besides Veronica. If he was going to lose the race, he'd rather lose to anyone else in class than her.

"Rats, rats, rats," he mumbled, hurrying home. He was wet and freezing from the drizzle that had begun to fall. On the way across the parking lot, he thought about trying the other apartment buildings, but someone in his class—or the other fourth grade—lived in each one.

If he'd been smart, he would have stayed home sick today, then spent the whole time selling peppermints.

You would've been caught, then lost your allowance for the rest of the year.

"I know, I know," he told himself.

Tony shivered, ducking his head under the hood of his jacket as he ran for the door. *I can't* afford *to lose my allowance. I have to pay for all the peppermints I keep buying. . . .*

7

Guitar Lessons

When Tony got home, Uncle John greeted him at the door. He was wearing a Burnt Spyders T-shirt, his hair pulled back into a short ponytail.

"Hey," he said, giving Tony a hug. "Sis invited me to dinner, so I brought my guitar and the Christmas music like I promised."

Sis was Tony's mom, Uncle John's sister.

During dinner they asked a million questions about the red guitar. Tony didn't know what to say. Should he warn them he might not win after all? Or should he try harder tomorrow to sell peppermints?

But to who?

After dinner he and his uncle sprawled on the couch to practice. "Remember how to finger the C chord?" Uncle John asked, crooking three fingers around the neck of his ancient guitar.

He played for a minute, then handed the instrument to Tony, helping him hold his fingers the correct way. "Now strum," Uncle John said.

Tony strummed. The chord sounded "off"—not clear, the way his uncle made it sound. Holding down strings was harder than it looked.

"Fingering chords will be easier on *your* guitar," Uncle John said. "The neck will be narrower, to fit your hand." He unzipped a softcover case and pulled out his small travel guitar. "In the meantime, you can borrow this to practice on."

Tony tried the C chord. The strings *were* easier to reach.

By bedtime he'd learned the chorus to "Jingle Bells" and "We Wish You a Merry Christmas."

Some chords were trickier than others. After a while his fingers became sore, so he had to stop. Uncle John showed him the calluses on his own fingertips from sliding them up and down the wire strings.

Tony's mom applauded his first concert. "Good job!" she said, aiming her camera. "Look here and smile."

Tony rose to his feet and crossed his arms, wiping the smile off his face. Just like the musicians in Toxic. Uncle John turned his back to Tony's and struck the same pose.

"You guys," Tony's mom groaned. "You don't look like you're having any fun."

"No, but we do look cool, right, Anthony?"

"Right, dude."

"That's *Uncle* Dude."

They waited until after the camera flashed to laugh.

Uncle John packed his guitar in its blue-velvet-lined case. "You're a quick learner," he said. "When will you know if you won the red guitar?"

"Friday," Tony answered. "But . . ." How should he break the news? "A few kids have sold more peppermints than I have, so I don't know if . . ." His voice trailed off. He didn't want to disappoint them.

"Can I take a box to work with me tomorrow?" his mother asked. "Maybe a few people in my office would like to buy Christmas candy."

"Yeah!" Tony felt excited. Why hadn't *he* thought of it?

"Hey, I'll ask the Spyders," Uncle John said. "They always have the munchies." He gave Tony a friendly nudge on the chin. "I'll call you tomorrow and tell you how many bags I sold."

"Thanks." Tony said good night, hurrying to his room to total today's sales. He took three dollars from his bank to pay for the candy he left at the Eldercare Center, then threw in one more and opened a bag for himself.

Twelve Xs. Twelve dollars. Fewer than yesterday.

Well, tomorrow would be better. Both Mom and Uncle John would help. And he'd just had a terrific brainstorm.

He'd ask Mom to drive him to Grandmother Adler's house to deliver the four bags she'd bought. She lived so far away, Tony could walk around her entire neighborhood, and no one would say, "Someone named Veronica already beat you here and sold us a zillion bags of peppermints."

It was a great idea.

8

Eighty Bags
and Counting

Dear Zelda Mask,

I have read seven of your books. I like them a lot. Now I am reading <u>Mystery of the Dragon King</u>. Why does Sir Perry have to spend so much time trying to free a stupid princess? Why does he have to kiss her?

Why can't he be like Sir Weslyn, the knight in <u>Battle of Seven Kingdoms</u>? He killed bad guys on every page. He went into the evil wizard's cave alone. In the dark. With snakes after him. That was so cool. He didn't kiss anybody. Please write back.

Your Reader,

Anthony Adler (Tony)

Tony glanced at the clock. Time for lunch. He folded the letter and slipped it into the stamped envelope Miss Kimball made them bring from home for their "Write an Author" assignment.

Neatly he printed Zelda Mask's name across the front.

Flipping open the book, he found the publisher's address, then copied it under the author's name.

As he set the letter on the teacher's desk, Veronica Tangle arrived, finally, from her morning doctor's appointment. Tony wondered if she'd sold peppermints to every doctor and nurse at the medical center.

Veronica handed a tardy slip and her candy envelope to Miss Kimball, then walked to her desk.

Tony followed. "May I have my dollar now?"

"What dollar?" Veronica wrinkled her pudgy nose the same way his gerbil did when Tony picked him up.

"The dollar you took from Mrs. Glenn for the candy I sold her."

"I already gave it to Miss Kimball."

"Well? Did you tell her?" Tony noticed how Veronica's wispy hair stuck up on top—also like his gerbil's. As a matter of fact, her hair was the same charcoal color as Toxic's—without the white splotches, of course.

"Tell her *what*?" Veronica asked.

He wondered if she was bluffing. "Did you tell her to count the dollar after my name?"

Veronica's smile took a long time to spread across her face. Tony half-expected her to have gerbil teeth in front—tiny and rectangular. But they were people teeth. "No," she said. "I didn't tell her it was your dollar."

"That's not fair." Tony's face heated in anger.

"Mrs. Glenn paid *me*, so *I* get credit."

"But *I* sold her the candy." He knew it wasn't quite the truth. Peter had ruined a bag. Mrs. Glenn simply paid for the damage.

Veronica narrowed her beady eyes at him. "Then you should have gotten the money right then and there."

"Please stop talking and take your seat," came Miss Kimball's voice.

Tony whirled away from Veronica's desk and stumbled to his own. "It's not fair," he repeated in a whisper. But there was no way he could force Miss Gerbil Head to give him a dollar. As if she needed it.

Slumping in his desk, he pictured Veronica with Toxic's head on her scrawny shoulders. "Gerbil Head, Gerbil Head, Gerbil Head," he muttered under his breath. It gave him great pleasure.

Tony squinted at the candy graph. One lonely peppermint followed his name. Big deal. Erica had two. So did Ann. Veronica now had three. Three! Tony would never catch up.

Before school he'd peeked into the other fourth grade to look at their candy graph. It wasn't as nifty as the one Erica and Ann had made—just a list of names with squiggly lines separating them. And the leader in that class lagged behind, with only two candy pieces.

Tony sighed. At least he was tied with most of the kids in both classes. And he was way ahead of Jeremy—the only one who had *no* candy taped after his name. He'd sold only seventeen bags.

Being ahead of Jeremy made Tony feel worse. Besides having so few neighbors, Jeremy had no grandparents. And the rest of his relatives lived in Canada.

On the way to lunch, Tony slipped into the library to take another peek at the red Starcatcher guitar. Jeremy was there ahead of him, gazing into the prize case.

"What are you doing?" Tony asked, pretending he'd stopped because his friend was there.

"Just looking." Jeremy backed away, flustered at being caught. "That skateboard is so much better than the one I had."

"The one you left in the alley?"

"Yeah. My dad told me to put it away before dinner— but I forgot." Jeremy made a scrunchy face. "By the time I finished eating, my skateboard was gone."

He touched the display case, like he was claiming his prize. "I really want to win this one."

Tony felt the same way about the red guitar.

"If only I could sell more peppermints," Jeremy added.

"Look," Tony began, feeling uncertain over the offer he was about to make. "Mom's taking me to my grandmother's tonight so I can sell peppermints in her neighborhood. Want to come?"

It'll be fewer sales for me, Tony told himself, *but it might earn Jeremy a candy piece on the graph*. Not having *any* pieces had to be embarrassing.

A grin lit Jeremy's face. "I'll ask my mom the *minute* I get home."

He dashed off toward the cafeteria, so Tony followed.

After school Tony could hardly wait for his mom to get home. He was waiting at the door when she arrived, a candy box in her gloved hand.

The box was almost empty of candy, but full of dollar bills.

Tony counted. Sixteen! Sixteen bags of peppermints sold! He quickly marked sixteen Xs on his envelope.

"Hooray!" he shouted, dancing around his mother while she struggled to get out of her coat.

After changing clothes, they left for Grandmother Adler's, picking up Jeremy—and a bag of hamburgers—along the way.

Tony's grandmother served dessert. She was dressed in a red jumpsuit decorated with green Christmas trees. Tiny lights on the trees blinked on and off. He thought it very unlike his grandmother to wear blinking clothes, but Jeremy thought it was cool, so Tony guessed it was too.

After eating cookies and fruitcake in the cozy, oven-warmed kitchen, Grandmother Adler paid Tony for the four bags, then changed her mind and bought two more.

Tony and Jeremy bundled into their jackets and started around the block, sharing houses to make it fair. Holiday decorations lit their way through the crisp December night.

In one block they received twelve *yeses*, ten *no thank yous*, eight barking dogs, two escaped cats, one scuffed shoe (Jeremy slid off a porch), one teenager who took the candy and never came back with the money, and one lady who tried to sell them candy from *her* son's school.

After that, they split up, going in different directions. Tony was getting real good at reciting his speech, since he'd done it so many times.

Business was fantastic. He *sold* all his candy—thirty-seven bags—then wished he'd brought another box from home. He never thought he'd be so lucky.

Hurrying back to his grandmother's, he met Jeremy along the way. "How'd you do?" Tony called.

"Great! I sold two whole boxes!"

"Wow." Tony reminded himself that those two boxes could *not* have been his, since he sold all he'd brought.

They counted their profits on the ride home. Today had netted Tony fifty-five sales in all. Better than Veronica Tangle on her first day.

Fifty-five added to sales from the last two days totaled eighty. Four pieces of candy would follow his name on the graph tomorrow, like four special Christmas presents.

Jeremy had sold forty bags. With his previous sales, it earned him two candy pieces, almost three.

Tony's mom bought a bag from Jeremy to share during the trip home. They had a contest to see who could make one piece last the longest. The winner, unfortunately, was his mother.

Still, the candy tasted good. It tasted sweet. It almost tasted like victory.

9

No Kissing Please

Tony loved the way classrooms smelled this time of year. Miss Kimball set a live fir tree on top of the bookshelf. The class strung popcorn and cranberry chains on the boughs, along with handmade paper ornaments decorated with glitter and fake snow.

Miss Kimball even let them play Christmas music in the afternoons, as long as they worked quietly and didn't talk too much.

This morning Tony's spirits were as high as the glittery star on top of the tree as he watched Erica and Ann tape peppermints to the candy graph. With four pieces next to his name, he was way ahead of the entire class.

Until they got to Veronica Tangle's name at the bottom.

Tony watched Erica and Ann add two more candy pieces. Now Veronica had five.

His stomach hurt—probably because he'd eaten a bag of candy instead of breakfast. Today was allowance day, so he had five more dollars to spend.

Of course, he'd rather spend his allowance on something other than peppermints.

Veronica flitted about the room, milking the attention of being the obvious winner. Miss Kimball had given her a *sixth* box of candy, so Veronica had sold well over a hundred bags.

Tomorrow was the last day before vacation. Prize day.

There was no way Tony could sell three whole boxes of candy before morning. Sixty bags.

What did it matter that Gerbil Head fudged on Tony's one measly dollar? He'd complained to Miss Kimball, and she agreed to subtract a dollar from Veronica's total and add it to his. Still, it didn't make him feel as good as he thought it would. One dollar wouldn't change anything now.

Tomorrow was also the day his class went Christmas caroling at the Eldercare Center. He felt excited about singing for Mr. Ramirez. Tony had told him about the

guitar lessons, but was glad he hadn't mentioned *winning* the guitar.

During library time Mr. Peek was beside himself. "Sit, sit," he ordered in his loud whisper.

The class sat in an uneven circle on the floor.

"The peppermint race has been so successful," Mr. Peek told them, "when you come back to school after holiday break, you won't recognize the library. The shelves will be filled with new titles."

The fourth graders clapped and cheered.

"Who wants to hand out my book survey?" he asked.

"Uh, uh," grunted Jeremy.

Mr. Peek handed the sheets to Jeremy. "The survey will tell me your favorite types of books so I can order what you like to read."

While Tony filled out his survey, Mr. Peek tapped him on the shoulder. "A new Zelda Mask book came in this morning," he whispered. "I kept it at the desk so you could be the first to have it."

A week ago Tony would have been thrilled. But after reading the *Dragon King* story, he vowed to take a good look at this new Zelda Mask book before checking it out. If there was kissing in it, well, he'd just have to find himself a new favorite author.

Browsing time was noisy today. Kids were hyper, since holiday break was so close. Mr. Peek had to remind them "This is a library" three times in twenty minutes.

Tony finished browsing. He took *Dragon King* to the checkout desk to turn it in, then asked to see the book Mr. Peek had saved for him.

"Look." He showed Tony the back flap. There was a picture of Zelda Mask, dressed in a full suit of armor. All that showed was her face.

Under the picture it read: *Zelda Mask, author of many mysteries for young readers, is now Zelda Mask Nekowski, following her recent marriage.*

"Her recent marriage?" Tony read out loud. *No wonder her last book was full of mush and kisses.*

He flipped to the cover. A knight in black armor brandished a sword in front of a two-headed creature rising from an angry sea. Blood dripped from the sword and the letters in the title: *Mystery of the Evil Serpent.*

Tony grinned. Now *that's* the kind of Zelda Mask book he liked to read. Maybe the mushiness was only temporary—while she was falling in love.

"I'll take it," he told Mr. Peek.

The librarian stamped the book, then handed him a

sealed envelope. "Will you deliver this note to Nancy—er—I mean, Miss Kimball?"

"Sure." Tony figured the librarian might enjoy Zelda Mask's mushiness a lot more than he did. He pointed to the *Dragon* book. "You should read this, Mr. Peek. There's some stuff in here I think you'll like."

That night Uncle John came by to listen to Tony practice. Tony was careful not to mention winning the red guitar.

Of course, if he stopped spending all his money on peppermints, maybe he could save enough to pay for a guitar of his own.

The Burnt Spyders had ordered nine bags of peppermints. Not enough to zoom Tony ahead of Veronica, but a sale was a sale.

After sacrificing the four remaining dollars from this week's allowance to the peppermint envelope, the day's total was fourteen. Same as his first day. Fourteen plus eighty-one equaled ninety-five.

It wasn't quite enough for one more candy piece on the graph, but it *was* enough for Mr. Peek to buy a whole lot of new books.

Before he went to bed, Tony let Toxic out of his cage

to wander around on his bedspread, looking for bits of lettuce. While he watched the gerbil, Tony polished off all four bags of candy.

Now his stomach ached. When he closed his eyes, all he saw were red-and-white candy-cane people dancing behind his eyelids. They all had gerbil heads and Veronica's skinny body.

Moaning, he put Toxic back into his cage and went to bed.

As he tossed and turned, Tony began to hate the sight and smell and taste and *feel* of peppermint candy.

He hated it so much, if he didn't eat another piece for a hundred zillion years, it would still be far too soon.

10

We Wish You
a Merry Christmas

Tony jolted awake.

In his dream, Sir Perry wore tiny glasses like Mr. Peek. As a matter of fact, he looked a lot like Mr. Peek, right down to his whisper-voice.

Behind the princess's veil glowed Miss Kimball's face.

Sir Perry grasped the princess's arm and yanked her out of the Dragon King's fiery path. Her high heels buckled and she began to fall, but Sir Perry pulled her onto his peppermint-striped steed and galloped to safety. Then he lifted her veil and kissed her.

In the middle of the kiss, the Dragon King rose up behind them with a terrible roar. He was playing a red guitar, singing Christmas songs in his screechy Veronica voice.

What a nightmare.

Before that, Tony had dreamed that Jeremy moved even farther away. To Canada. And Tony never saw his friend again.

He shuddered. It was *not* going to be a fun day.

Tony had five bags of peppermints to return to Miss Kimball out of the hundred he'd been assigned. He didn't want to return any.

Shaking five dollars from his football bank, he counted his remaining Christmas money. Two dollars and fifteen cents. Well, he'd just have to borrow money from his mother for Jeremy's present.

On the way to school Tony stopped at the Eldercare Center. Few people were around this early. He stepped into the reception room and emptied all five bags of peppermints into the holiday bowl.

"Merry Christmas," he whispered.

School started with art class while final sales for both fourth grades were tallied. It was hard to concentrate on coloring holiday cards while waiting for the big announcement.

Finally it was time. Both classes were herded to the library for the fourth grade awards ceremony. Mr. Peek gave a thank-you speech, then announced the top salesperson. It was no big deal, really, since everyone knew it was Veronica Tangle.

After the applause, Mr. Peek unlocked the glass doors of the display case and asked Veronica to select her prize.

Tony tried not to watch, but he did. Veronica took her time browsing through the prizes, just for show. Then she picked up the Starcatcher guitar and the Pig-nose amp and carried them back to her place.

The fourth grade clapped again. Except for Tony. He tried to be happy about all the new books the library could buy now, but . . . but he *really* wanted that guitar.

The rest of the winners chose prizes one by one. A few came from the other fourth grade, but most were from Tony's class. Erica picked the Rollerblades. Ann chose a Benetton Barbie.

"To-ny," Jeremy hissed, poking him in the side.

"Huh?"

"They called your name."

"They did?"

"Tony Adler," Mr. Peek repeated. "Come select your prize."

Tony hadn't thought about winning any prize other than the guitar. He was pleased to find himself in the winner's circle, but none of the prizes in the case appealed to him.

"*Choose*," Mr. Peek told him. "We've got to be at the Eldercare Center in thirty minutes."

Suddenly Tony knew exactly what he wanted. He chose the skateboard. It would be a hard gift to wrap, and he'd probably make a terrible mess of it, but he didn't think Jeremy would notice.

Tony and Jeremy held the double doors open at the Eldercare Center while the class filed in. Risers had been set up at one end of the reception area. The class took their places. Tallest in back; shortest in front.

The worst part of all was that Tony had to stand next to Veronica. She'd brought the guitar and amp with her, which only made Tony feel more miserable.

Mr. Peek had come along to help, or so he said. Tony thought it was so he could sit next to Miss Kimball on the piano bench while she played Christmas carols. All he did was turn pages of the songbook.

"*Jingle bells, jingle bells, jingle all the way. . . .*"

The sound of singing drew senior citizens out of their rooms and into the reception area. After a few songs Mr. Ramirez appeared. He stepped up to the risers and shook Tony's hand. Tony felt embarrassed at being singled out.

One of the ladies sat at a small organ in the back of the room and joined in with her version of "Jingle Bells." Soon a man appeared with two guitars and handed one to Mr. Ramirez.

"Wow," Tony whispered. Mr. Ramirez? Playing the guitar?

Another lady went to her room, then returned with a small xylophone so she could play along too. A tall man with a beard pulled a harmonica from his jacket pocket and joined in the holiday song.

When the music stopped, everyone clapped for each other.

Then Mr. Ramirez held out his guitar to Tony. "Show us what you've learned," he said.

Tony's heart stopped. Was he serious?

"Why, Tony," Miss Kimball exclaimed. "I didn't know you could play."

Tony stepped off the risers and sat in a chair. He laid Mr. Ramirez's guitar across his lap. This guitar was big, even bigger than Uncle John's. Stretching his fingers around the neck, he tried to strum a clear chord.

But his fingers weren't long enough.

Tony's face burned. "I can't play," he said to Miss Kimball. "The neck is too wide for my hand."

He gave the guitar back to Mr. Ramirez with a shrug. His heart was pounding as fast as his gerbil's tiny heart.

"You can use *my* guitar," Veronica chirped as Tony made his way to the third step on the riser.

He stopped and stared at her, thankful he'd never called her Gerbil Head to her face.

She smiled, lifting the amp over the row of kids in front of her. "Just plug it in."

The class clapped, cheering him on.

Tony didn't need a second invitation. He plugged the amp in next to the piano, then strapped on the guitar the way Uncle John had taught him. Mr. Ramirez helped him tune the strings until they were in key.

Then Tony sat down and played on the candy-apple-red guitar:

"We wish you a Merry Christmas. . . ."

After one line, everyone joined in—Miss Kimball on piano (with Mr. Peek sitting much too close, as far as Tony was concerned), Mr. Ramirez and his friend on guitar, the organist, the xylophone player, the harmonica player, and the fourth grade carolers:

"We wish you a Merry Christmas and a Happy New Year!"